·DRIBBLES·

For Genevieve and Maxie—C.H.
For Grandpa Weinstein and Zanny the Cat—E.S.

Clarion Books
a Houghton Mifflin Company imprint
215 Park Avenue South, New York, NY 10003
Text copyright © 1993 by Connie Heckert
Illustrations copyright © 1993 by Elizabeth Sayles

Printed in the U.S.A.

Library of Congress Cataloging-in-Publication Data
Heckert, Connie K.
Dribbles / by Connie Heckert ; illustrated by Elizabeth Sayles.
p.   cm.
Summary: The family cats work hard at befriending the new,
though elderly, cat that moves in with the family's grandfather, and are
especially glad they did when that cat dies knowing it was loved.
ISBN 0-395-62336-7
[1. Cats—Fiction.   2. Death—Fiction.   3. Old age—Fiction.]
I. Sayles, Elizabeth, ill.   II. Title.
PZ7.H3544Dr   1993
[E]—dc20   92-24846   CIP   AC

BP 10 9 8 7 6 5 4 3 2 1

· D R I B B L E S ·

by Connie Heckert ◆ Illustrated by Elizabeth Sayles

CLARION BOOKS · NEW YORK

Bing, Benny, and Gracie watched the old man as he sat in his chair, head bowed. The room was hushed like the world outside where fresh snow had fallen. They whispered, almost afraid to break the silence.

"Who is that old man?" Benny asked. Benny wore a yellow collar.

"You know," Bing said to his brother. Bing always said, "You know," even when he didn't. He had a red collar, the color of Bing cherries.

"Yes, you do," Gracie told the Siamese kittens. She was older, black and white with a small, delicate head. "It's the old man. You saw him at Christmas with the old woman. She pulled him around everywhere, like a wagon, because he walked so slow. Now she has died and he is alone."

"But who is the stranger?" Benny asked. "Why has she moved in with us? This is our home."

The stranger, a very old cat, had a coat of amber colors. It was long, full of snarls and mats. When Benny rubbed against her, she hissed and spat, "Hhhckkt," then ran under the old man's bed.

"So why is she here?" Benny asked again. "She's not friendly."

"You know," Bing said. He turned to Gracie for an answer.

"She lived with the old man and woman," Gracie said. "They gave up on brushing her coat."

"I can tell," said Benny. "It's a mess."

The three watched as their people went toward the old man's bed. They could smell toast and hot coffee. The man pulled the stranger out from under the bed. Her tail swished back and forth as she hissed and spat, "Hhhckkt!"

"She's not friendly," Bing said.

Benny gave Bing a funny look. "I already said that."

"Not like us." Bing nudged Gracie with affection.

"I agree," said Gracie. "The man calls her Dribbles. How could she have gotten such a name?"

"Maybe she's messy," said Benny.

When the man put Dribbles down, her tail still swishing, she ran back under the bed and huddled there, looking out.

Time after time, Benny sauntered into the guest room where the old man sat looking out the window at the white winter day. He approached the strange Dribbles. And again she hissed and spat, "Hhhckkt."

Bing laughed at his brother. "You know, Benny," Bing said, "I'm glad you don't give up."

"That's me. I don't give up."

That night the three cats slept at the foot of the old man's bed. Gracie was awake, licking her black and white coat, when Dribbles went to her dish to drink and eat. Gracie watched as the old cat explored the room where she and the old man now lived. Dribbles jumped on the bed where he slept. The old man awoke. He reached out to pet her, talking softly, and she purred.

The next morning, Bing and Benny raced off to play.

Benny chased Bing from one end of the house to the other. Up the stairs. Down the stairs. Over the chairs. In front and behind curtains and through the tunnel behind the sofa. Until finally, Gracie couldn't stand it any longer. "Stop it!" she screeched.

They skidded to a halt, then lay on the floor, looking up at Gracie. That's where they were when the woman brought the old cat, with her coat of amber colors, from the guest room. The woman put Dribbles in a pet carrier and went out to the car.

"Where do you think they're going?" Benny asked.

"You know," Bing said. He looked to Gracie for an answer.

Gracie nodded wisely. "To the vet's," she said and shuddered.

Later the woman and Dribbles returned. Bing, Benny, and Gracie stared with shock. The tail was still bushy, and the face was furry. But the long coat of amber colors was gone. It had been sheared next to the skin like a baby lamb's.

"She's so skinny," said Benny. "I wish I could ask her my question."

"You knew she was tiny," said Bing. He looked at Gracie.

"Not me," said Gracie. "You can see the bumps on her backbone. She walks like the old man." Gracie shook her head. "No questions, Benny. Not yet."

Over and over, Benny kept trying to make friends. Gracie and Bing watched as he strolled toward Dribbles. Each time she hissed and spat, and struck out with her paw as if to say, "Keep away." Then she ran off to hide.

As time passed, the snow melted and spring turned to summer. Dribbles came out more. She watched for danger and ran if approached too quickly. Bing and Benny knew she was there as they tumbled with a toy mouse. She began to eat in the kitchen with the others.

Now, when the man or woman picked her up, she was quiet before she began to hiss. One day, as the sun shone, she purred. Benny rubbed against her, and she licked his neck.

Now the brothers, Gracie, and Dribbles all slept at the foot of the old man's bed. Three together and one apart.

Once they were friends, Gracie told Benny he could ask the old cat his question. Benny wasted no time.

"Why were you so nasty?" He nudged her with affection. "We're family."

"Family? Nasty?" Dribbles asked, amused. "My life changed from everything I knew. The old woman didn't come home. Now the old man hangs his head. And my warm coat, with pretty amber colors, is gone."

Gracie nodded. "I was sad for a long time after my brother George went away."

"Where did he go?" asked Benny. This was a new story.

"We don't know," she said. "He left one cold night and didn't come back. The man and woman searched for days."

"Like the old woman?" the old cat asked.

"Maybe," said Gracie.

"Why was it sad?" Benny asked.

"Goodbyes are always sad," said Dribbles. "Especially when you don't get to say them."

Gracie nodded, licking her black and white coat.

More and more, Dribbles shared time with her new family. She watched as Gracie and the kittens chased popcorn. She curled up in front of the window where the crab apple tree outside was thick with pink blossoms. Sometimes Dribbles watched a mother wren feed her young.

One day Dribbles didn't feel well, and she didn't come out of the old man's bedroom. The man and the woman went to pick Dribbles up. They put her gently on a cushion and carried her to the family room, laying her on the floor in the sunshine. The woman ran her hand gently over the short, soft coat. She fed Dribbles water with an eyedropper.

Benny sauntered over and nudged Dribbles with his nose. The old cat gave a soft cry. For once, Benny didn't know what to say.

"Why is she sick?" he asked Bing.

"You know," said Bing.

"No, I don't," Benny snapped. "And I wish you'd stop saying that."

Gracie didn't laugh. "I have a sad feeling," she said. "Like I do in the fall when the gold and brown leaves drop from the trees before the snows come. And the ground turns cold."

"Should we say goodbye?" asked Benny.

Gracie nodded.

So the three of them went to Dribbles's side and sat there. Benny licked the old cat's cheek. "I'm glad we're friends," he said to Dribbles.

"Me, too," said Bing.

She nodded and purred ever so quietly.

All day the friends sat close to Dribbles. They didn't play, and they talked in whispers. When the day faded to a soft silver twilight, they watched as the silent Dribbles was wrapped in cloths and carried out the door for the last time.

"Why did she have to die?" Benny asked quietly.

Gracie looked at Bing in his red collar, and Benny in his yellow one. Her eyes, too, were sad.

"I think life is like that. All living things are born and live until they die," said Gracie. "She knew we loved her. I feel better because we were friends and had time to say goodbye."

"Yes, but why did Dribbles have to die?"

"You know," said Bing.

And they did.